STORIES FROM CANTERBURY PLACE

THE BIG GREEN TREE AT NO. 11

TAMMY AND JAKE
LEARN ABOUT LIFE AND DEATH

CATHERINE MACKENZIE

Published by Christian Focus Publications Ltd
Geanies House, Tain, Ross-shire, IV20 1TW
©2002 Christian Focus Publications

Cover Illustration by Dave Thomson Bee
Hive Illustration. All other illustrations by
Chris Rothero Bee Hive Illustration.

Printed and bound in Great Britain by
Cox and Wyman, Reading
ISBN 1-85792-731-1

For
Marianne
and
Wilma

~

with thanks and love

~

Catherine

A Map of Canterbury Place

The Church

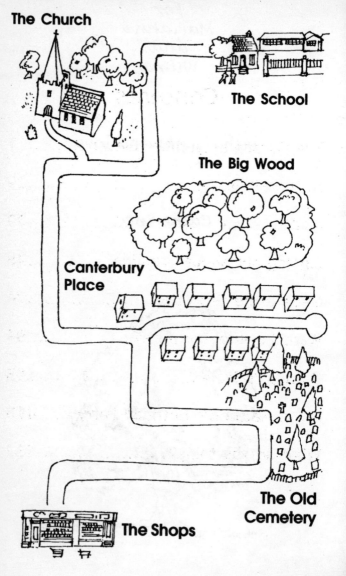

The School

The Big Wood

Canterbury Place

The Old Cemetery

The Shops

Contents

The Garden at Number Eleven

The MacDonalds lived at Number Eleven, Canterbury Place in a lovely house, with a big back garden. Mr and Mrs MacDonald had two children, Jake and Tammy. Jake was the oldest. He was eight years old, with toffee-brown hair and eyes to match. Jake quite liked school except for spelling which he wasn't very good at. Maths was his best subject. He always got top marks.

But now it was the holidays. The sun was in the sky, there was no classes to go to and Jake was quite pleased he could do what he liked for a while.

Tammy, Jake's little sister, had pale blue eyes and soft golden hair but she wasn't quite five years old, she was only four.

However Mum kept reminding Tammy that it wouldn't be long before she was five years old and then she would have a birthday party.

Tammy couldn't wait. She was longing to be five years old.

Jake was longing to be nine years old. He wanted to be old enough to hang around with the big boys like Dave Johnson who lived at number twelve.

Dave Johnson had roller blades and sped off down the road at a great speed. Jake longed to be able to do this. Jake longed to be nine years old. Dad kept reminding Jake that he would have to be patient.

Jake didn't like being patient. He always wanted things to happen immediately.

One morning Tammy and Jake were playing in the garden. The sun was shining above them and glinting at them through the leaves of the big green tree that grew in the back garden.

An old tyre had been attached to some rope and then tied onto one of the big, strong branches of the big, green tree. Jake loved to sit in the middle of the tyre and swing out from the tree. If he was feeling very brave he would ask his dad to twist the rope, round and round and then let go. Jake would go spinning in circles. He would go so fast that his eyes went squint and his tummy squirmy.

Jake thought that it was great to have such a big green tree in their garden. No other garden in Canterbury place had a tree as big as theirs.

Jake and Tammy looked at their big green tree. It was towering above them. It had lots of leaves, hundreds and thousands of them. It was a special tree.

Dogger, Tammy and Jake's dog, was sniffing around at the roots of the tree. There were lots of interesting smells in the garden and Dogger was having a great time.

"What are you smelling Dogger? Is it a cat? Where is it then?"

Dogger, who still behaved like a great big puppy, started running around barking. "Silly, scruffy, dog," Jake laughed.

Jake reached out and tickled Dogger behind the ears, just where he liked it. Dogger smiled and closed his eyes, his pink tongue hanging out from his mouth.

Tammy stared up at the branches and leaves of the big green tree and looked to see if she could spot the bird's nest her dad had told her about. Tammy loved the big green tree. She loved the shiny leaves, she loved the way the birds sat on the branches and sang. Tammy loved the big green tree.

Jake liked it too, it had a swing, it had huge branches and it was the biggest tree by far in the whole area - but he liked it better when it was autumn.

Jake loved autumn. He loved the way the great big tree let its leaves fall down, down, down onto the grass. Hundreds of leaves fluttered in the breeze and then on a Saturday afternoon Jake's dad would say, "Right, Autumn's here. It's time to brush up those dead leaves."

Jake and his dad would then put on their hats and coats and pull on their gloves and go into the garden to brush up the dead leaves.

But now that spring was here all the crunchy dead leaves had gone and the great big tree was all green again.

When the spring time came the great big tree grew hundreds of brand new little leaves. Tammy thought the green leaves looked like a lovely new dress. She was sure that the tree must like it's new leaves.

"I like the green tree best," she said.

Jake thought a little. He liked the green tree, but he still preferred autumn.

"I love the crunchy sound you make when you jump in the middle of all the leaves. I love the swish, swish noise you make when you kick your feet into a great big pile of leaves. I especially like the leaves and their bright golden red colours."

Tammy thought a little, she was sure she liked the green leaves best. They looked so fresh and clean. They reminded her of minty chews because they were so green. But they didn't taste minty. She had tried tasting a leaf last week - and had spat it out on the grass with a "Yuck!"

Tammy then remembered something. "The green leaves are alive. The brown leaves are dead. Why do things die Jake?" asked Tammy, puzzled.

Jake thought long and hard.

It was a hard question. Jake had to

think really long and really hard. He thought so long and so hard that his head hurt. This was a really difficult question.

He looked at the big green tree. He wasn't sure if that was really alive. It didn't do much in the garden except stand there, still and quiet.

Jake then spotted a bird singing in the branches. Tammy asked, "Will that bird die one day?"

Jake nodded his head, "I'm sure it will," he said sadly. "If that bird was dead, it wouldn't move, sing or eat. It wouldn't do anything. It would just fall out of its tree."

Tammy frowned a little. She didn't like thinking about it. But she was still puzzled about death.

"What happens then?" she asked

Jake didn't know how to answer any of Tammy's questions so he ran inside to speak to his mum and Tammy followed him.

In the Kitchen

The kitchen at Number Eleven was always in a bit of a muddle. Mum kept all the papers, bills and receipts in a large pile beside the telephone.

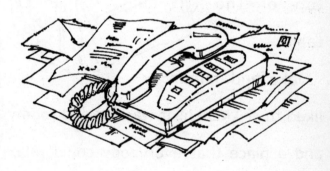

Pictures and photos and other interesting bits and pieces were stuck all over the refrigerator.

Dogger's basket was in the corner and Jake's school bag was dumped underneath the table. Tammy didn't have a school bag as she hadn't started school yet. But Tammy's crayons and a big pad of paper were sitting on top of the table.

Jake and Tammy liked their kitchen. It was big and roomy and a place that everybody could relax in.

When they got inside, Jake went to the refrigerator for a cool drink of orange juice and Tammy went up to Mum to ask her question.

"Mum," asked Tammy. "What happens to a bird when it's dead?"

Mum thought a little and said, "When a bird dies its body stops working. It falls to the ground and then little by little the bird's body turns into dust. The little bird's body doesn't stay the same for ever. All bodies when they die turn into dust. All animals, birds, people. Everything and everyone dies some day."

Tammy looked a little worried. She felt a little sad. She felt sad for the little bird on the branch outside. She didn't want the little bird to die. She didn't want it to stop singing.

Jake looked a little worried too. He didn't

want to die. He didn't want to stop living.

Mum looked at their faces and smiled. She could tell that something was worrying them. Giving them both a hug she asked Tammy and Jake what was the matter. Tammy whispered, "I feel sorry for the little bird outside. Will it die?"

"Yes," said her mum. "All animals die. But I'll tell you a story about a little bird."

Mum sat down at the kitchen table and moving Tammy's crayons to one side she told Tammy and Jake a story.

"This is a story about a little bird and a very special man. His name is Jesus. He was born a long time ago. Can you tell me why he is special?"

Tammy thought and Jake did too. Jake said, "Was it because he was very good?"

"Yes, Jesus was very good but he is special for another reason. Jesus is special because he is the Son of God. He has never done anything wrong. Well, one day Jesus saw a little sparrow. Someone had it in a cage. It was going to be sold along with all its brothers and sisters. Two of these sparrows were sold for one penny and Jesus saw it. Then he told his friends something wonderful about God. He told them that whenever a little sparrow falls to the ground God knows about it.

"So you don't have to worry about the

little birds who die. God knows all about them. God made all the little birds and the animals. He gives them their food and shelter when they are alive so we don't have to worry about them when they die."

Tammy smiled, she wouldn't worry about her little bird anymore.

Jake still looked worried though so his mum gave him another hug and ruffled the top of his toffee-brown hair.

"What's troubling you Jake? You can tell me."

Jake whispered to his mum, "What will happen to me when I die? You said that I am going to die."

Jake's mum nodded, "Well when Jesus

told the story about the little birds he also spoke about people. He said that when little birds fall to the ground God knows about it. But he also said that people who love and trust in God are worth much more than a couple of sparrows. God takes even more care of them.

If you love and trust in God he will protect you so much that you don't need to be afraid of dying anymore."

Before Jake could ask a question about that Jake's mum said something else.

"Of course one thing you have to remember is that dying is different for people. People are not the same as animals and birds. All men and women, boys and girls die but they have something different inside them that goes on living."

Jake shouted out, "I remember what that is! It's your soul!" he shouted out.

"That's right Jake. It's something called a soul, or a spirit. It's the bit inside you that you can't see, or touch, but that lives inside you all the same. It's the bit that makes you special, it makes you a human being. God gave people souls when he made the very first people. Can you remember the names of the very first people?" Mum asked.

Tammy thought a little and then she remembered.

"Adam and Eve. That's their names. Adam was the man and Eve was the lady."

"That's right!" Mum said, smiling, "And if you both go and get your coats we will go shopping and I will tell you what happens to you when you die."

Jake and Tammy ran to get their coats and mum went to get her hand-bag.

"My car wouldn't start this morning so we are going to have to go on the bus."

Tammy and Jake cheered as they struggled into their coats. They loved going on the bright red bus into town. There was always lots to see out the windows.

"We're going to have to rush if we're going to get the number nine bus." Mum reminded them. "Hurry up you two, we can't dilly dally."

But Jake and Tammy were already standing waiting for Mum at the door.

"We're ready Mum!" they both yelled.

A Journey on a Bus

At the road side Tammy held on to her mum's hand as they waited to cross to the bus stop. Jake stood by Mum's side holding the shopping bag. He was bigger and didn't have to hold anyone's hand. Tammy was still little and Mum didn't want her crossing the busy road on her own.

As the cars streamed past, with their wheels turning ever so fast Jake looked and looked. Would they ever get across this busy road he wondered. Red cars, blue cars, big cars, fast cars, all sped by. Tammy was a bit frightened, though she didn't let on. But Jake's mum looked at her and knew she felt a little scared.

"It's all right Tammy. We won't cross the road here, it's too busy. You've been learning about road safety haven't you? Where should we go to cross the road then?"

Tammy grinned, she knew the answer to that question. "We go to the traffic lights and wait for the green man."

"That's right. When the green man comes the cars stop and then we can walk across the road."

As they walked up to the traffic lights Tammy grinned again, "The cars are stopping now. The green man has come and we can cross the road safely."

Jake smiled to himself. He knew all about crossing roads. He could even tell you the names of the cars that zoomed by - Audi's, Mini's, Fiat's, Fords - he knew them all. But he remembered that Tammy was only little and just starting to learn about traffic and roads and things.

Jake walked across the road smartly, beside his mum and when they arrived at the bus stop everyone got a sweet from Mum. They were jelly babies, Jake's favourite. Mum then asked Jake a question.

"Were you frightened of the cars and the busy road Jake?"

Jake nearly choked on his jelly baby. "Me? Scared? Of course not! I know all about roads and how to cross them! Tammy was scared, I wasn't."

"I wasn't scared," complained Tammy.

"I'm sure you were both fine," sighed Mum, "but sometimes crossing a busy road is scary - I was just thinking that it's a bit like dying. For some people it can be scary. But for some people it isn't."

"Why does dying have to be scary?" asked Tammy, slightly annoyed. She didn't like scary things.

"Well some people are always scared of something that they don't know or understand. Some people are scared of dying because they aren't ready to die.

"You see, when God made the world he made it perfect. Nothing ever went wrong. The animals never went hungry, there was always plenty of food. Little birds never fell sick and died because there was no illnesses.

"God made Adam and Eve perfect too. When God made the world there wasn't any death at all. It didn't exist."

"Then what happened," asked Jake. "What made death?"

"I suppose you could say that people made death," sighed Mum "because they disobeyed God and listened to the devil instead.

"The devil, some people call him Satan, is evil. He is very wrong. He is the worst. He hated God so much that he wanted to hurt him. He hated to see Adam and Eve so happy that he wanted to do something to destroy them. So he told them a lie. He told them to do something that God had told them not to do. Do you remember what that was?"

Jake and Tammy shook their heads.

Mum smiled and gave them another sweet, "I'm sure you do really, but I'll tell you about it all the same. God had told Adam and Eve when he first made the garden of Eden that they were allowed to eat fruit from all the trees in the garden, except for one. That tree had a special name. It was called the Tree of Knowledge of Good and Evil. It was important that Adam and Eve did not eat any of the fruit from that tree.

"But the devil came one day, disguised as a snake, and he told Eve that she should eat it. She listened to the snake and thought about it. She saw that the fruit looked good and that it was good to eat and then she decided to do it. She decided to ignore God's instructions and disobey his commands. She ate the fruit."

"Oh, oh!" said Tammy.

"Yes, it was bad news. Do you know what she did next? She told Adam to eat it. And he did."

"Oh, oh! They're in trouble," said Tammy.

"That's right. They were. That is when sin came into the world and everything started to go wrong. Eve did it first, then Adam and that was when death began."

"This is a sad story," grumbled Tammy. "I don't like it."

"It is a sad story, Tammy," said Mum quietly. "God was upset with Adam and Eve. They had disobeyed him."

"Was he really angry, Mum?" asked Jake. "Did he give them a telling off?"

"He did give them a telling off. They shouldn't have disobeyed him. The rule was that because they disobeyed God they had to be punished.

"First of all God told them that they weren't allowed into the Garden of Eden ever again. They had to leave their home. But there were other punishments too.

"All of a sudden life became very, very, hard. Adam and Eve felt pain for the first time, they felt sad and lonely. They weren't close to God anymore. Everything had gone wrong.

"Adam and Eve started to grow old. Horrible things started happening.

"The animals were no longer their friends. Animals and birds even died. Everything had been lovely before. Now it was really horrible.

"Adam and Eve would get angry with each other. They would sometimes squabble. Adam and Eve had two little boys and the little boys would be naughty and misbehave too.

"Then one day Adam and Eve's son Cain killed his brother, Abel. That was a very sad day."

"That's awful!" exclaimed Jake.

"Yes. Adam and Eve must have been very sad. But then God still loved them even though they had disobeyed him. He still loved them even though he had punished them. And there had been that promise he had made them..."

"What promise was that Mum? You didn't tell us about a promise?"

"Didn't I? Well, on the day that Adam and Eve disobeyed God, he had to give them their punishment. But he also promised them that one day someone would come to defeat death and the devil.

"Adam and Eve were promised that one day a rescuer would come. Many years later, a long, long time after Adam and Eve had died, Jesus Christ was born. God's Son became a human being and he was God's special rescuer."

"But what has all this got to do with death Mum? I'm a bit confused!" Jake didn't know what to think.

"Well when Jesus lived on earth he didn't do anything wrong. Do you remember I told you that at home this morning?"

"Yes, I remember."

"Well, it's like this. People sinned and kept on sinning and just couldn't live a perfect life however hard they tried. Even very good people who loved and trusted God were always doing wrong things.

"The punishment for all this sin was death and not being able to be friends with God, ever. But God wanted to give people a second chance. He wanted people to come back and be friends with him again. So somebody had to live a perfect life, never sinning once, and then that person had to die. He would have to die instead of all the people who deserved to die."

Jake was amazed. God's plan was wonderful.

"So that's what Jesus did then Mum? He came to earth and never did a wrong thing, not even once, and then God punished him instead of us! Why?"

"He did it because he loves us. So that's why I am not afraid of dying."

Tammy looked amazed. "Why aren't you afraid of dying? Isn't it scary?"

Mum rummaged around in her bag for a moment and gave everyone another jelly baby, then she explained. "It's not scary because I trust in Jesus. I know that I don't have to be punished by God because I believe in Jesus Christ. I trust

Jesus. When you know that God has forgiven you, because Jesus took your punishment instead of you, then you know that you will go to heaven when you die.

"In heaven you will be with God and Jesus Christ for ever. Instead of being separated from God forever, when you die you will be with him forever and everything will be perfect once again. You will live forever with God and with all the people who love God. Heaven is a very special place.

"There is no wickedness there, only joy and love and peace. There is no anger or fighting or pain. The people who love and trust Jesus really want to go there so that they can be with him forever."

Tammy smiled. She liked the sound of that. Jake looked at the busy road once again. He looked at the other people on the other side of the road. Mum pointed at the busy road.

"When you don't love and trust God, death is scary. It's a bad thing. It's like you are on one side of a very busy road and God is on the other and there isn't any way of getting across to him.

"But when you trust in Jesus Christ and ask him to forgive you for the wrong things you have done, when you die God will help and look after you. When you love

Jesus you don't need to be frightened of death. When you are crossing a road, it is safe to cross when the green man is there. When you die, if you trust in Jesus, you will be safe.

"Trusting in Jesus is the only way to be friends with God again and the only way to get to heaven when you die... but we have been waiting a long time for this bus. Can you see it anywhere Jake? It must be late."

Jake jumped up from his seat and peered down the road. In the distance he saw a bright red bus, trundling up the road.

"I can see it Mum, I can see it. It's just coming round the corner."

Quickly Jake's mum looked out some money to pay the driver. The bus slowed down and the large electric doors swung open to let them on.

"Quick Jake, jump on and find us some nice seats to sit on," Mum said while she counted out the exact change for the bus fair. "Two children and one adult please," Mum said to the driver as Jake dashed up the bus to find some good seats.

There were some good seats half way up the bus - where Jake and Tammy could look out the window at the passing cars. Tammy and Jake pressed their noses up against the window pane as the bus sped down the road.

Finding out about Grandpa

As the bus turned round corners, and stopped at bus-stops Jake thought long and hard. He ran his fingers through his hair and scratched his head a little. Death was quite a puzzling thing to think about.

It was amazing how God had made the world perfect but then it was horrible about how people had mucked everything up and how the devil had made things all nasty and horrible.

Jake thought about all the times he fell out with his friends at school, about the time he had hit Tammy and about the time he had lied to Mum about the

broken vase. Mum still thought it was
Dogger that had knocked it over. Jake

felt horrible about that. A nasty feeling

wriggled about inside him whenever he

thought about the broken vase. He knew

that he should do the right thing and tell

Mum the truth but he couldn't quite bring

himself to do it. So he ignored the feeling

and tried to think about something else.

Suddenly Tammy spotted something on the other side of the road. Jake looked up and noticed that Tammy was pointing at a church.

"Is it a wedding Mum? Is it?"

A lot of people had gathered outside the church across the road. There were a lot of cars there and a policeman was directing the traffic.

The policeman stood out in the middle of the road and stopped the red bus from going any further. Then a big black car drove out from the church and some other cars followed it.

In the back of the big black car was a shiny wooden box. Jake couldn't see any sign of a bride or groom. It certainly wasn't a wedding.

Jake's mum said quietly that it was a funeral.

"What's a funeral?" asked Tammy.

"Some people have a funeral when a person dies. They go to a church or a

special building and have a quiet get-together. They might say thank you to God for the person."

"That's a nice thing to do. But why are all the people there wearing the same colour? Lots of them are wearing black. It looks really strange." Tammy's nose was pressed up against the window pane once more as she looked out on the strange scene.

Her mum began to explain, "Sometimes the people wear black clothes when they go to a funeral. This is just to show that they are sad.

"But some people wear bright clothes instead of black. They don't want to think about sad memories. They just want to think about the happy times they had with the person.

"Some people look sad at funerals and are quiet. But others are chatty and smile or joke. It's different for everyone. Some people miss their friend so much that they cry. Some people keep remembering the funny things that their friend said once or the good times that they had, so they laugh."

Mum peered out the window, too, as the cars drove past.

"I have been to funerals where the people thank God for the dead person's life. They also thank God for the good things the person did and for how that person showed people how lovely God was. They thank God that their friend is in heaven. Then they bury the person in the ground in a place called a cemetery."

Tammy looked puzzled. "Is a funeral a nice thing or not?"

Mum thought for a bit. "A funeral is sometimes a nice thing and sometimes it's not. When a friend or someone in your family has died having a funeral is a good thing to do. Often when a friend or relative dies you will feel sad. But when you have a funeral it is a special time to stop and talk to God about your feelings. You can get love and support from other people who miss your friend too. You can cry together if you want to."

"It's babyish to cry," Jake said.

"Not always. Babies cry a lot but adults and children can cry too. It's good to cry when something sad has happened.'

"I don't think I've ever been to a cemetery?" Jake said, feeling curious.

"If you look out the window in a little bit, you will see what a cemetery looks like. That's the place where your Grandpa is buried.

"When Grandpa died, before you were born, we had a church service like that one. We sang some songs, we prayed and read a bit from the Bible. Then we took Grandpa's body, which was in a big box called a coffin, and we buried him underneath the ground. I cried a bit because I felt sad. But look now, all the cars have moved on and the bus has started again."

The bus turned a corner and drove past a lovely little country lane. Mum looked out the window as if she was searching for somewhere.

"It should be near here," she muttered quietly. "Ah yes, there it is. Tammy lean across and press the red button for me darling. We're going to stop off early. There's somewhere I want to show you."

Tammy pressed the red button and the bus screeched to a halt at the bus stop. Mum thanked the bus driver. The bus doors opened wide. Then she took Tammy by the hand and pointed at something across the road.

"This is the cemetery where your Grandpa is buried. You'll be interested to see this place. It's quite special."

Jake and Tammy held Mum's hand as they crossed the road.

"Is this where that black car was coming to?" Jake asked, "I can't see it anywhere?"

Jake's mum looked around. "I can't see it either. They must have gone somewhere else. People don't often get buried in this cemetery now, it's getting full up."

Across the street was an old iron gate. The hinges squeaked as they opened it but as they walked in through the gates they saw rows and rows of grave stones.

"It looks like a farmer's field but it's very tidy. All these stones are laid out in lines," Jake looked around a bit more.

Some of the stones were very old and some were quite new. Some of the new grave stones had bright flowers in vases. One or two even had a large pile of flowers laid out on the grass just in front of the stone.

"The flowers are left there by the dead person's friends and relatives," explained Mum. "After the funeral is over some people like to show how they loved that person by leaving flowers beside the grave.

"Sometimes family and friends like to visit the grave stone to make sure that the grave is tidy and that there is always a vase of fresh flowers there to make the place look pretty."

Tammy smiled, "I think that's a nice idea. I like bright flowers." Tammy thought that the colourful flowers were like rainbows splashed all over the grass.

There were one or two very old statues

too and all the stones had writing on them. Jake read some as they walked along. Every stone had a name on it and two dates. One date for when the person had been born and the other date for when the person died. Sometimes there were other names as well - names of wives and sons and daughters who wanted people to know that they loved the person who was buried there.

"Grandpa's grave is this way," said Mum.

A couple of minutes later Mum stopped in front of a grey stone with writing on it.

"Jacob Frances Taylor, born 1930, died 1991. A loving husband to Martha and father to Jane and Matthew."

Jake looked at the stone and read the words out slowly.

"You're named after Grandpa, Jake. Martha is Grandma's name."

"Jane is your name and that's Uncle Matthew isn't it," said Jake.

"That's right. And this is where we buried Grandpa, my daddy. We were sad that he wasn't here any more because we missed him. But we were glad that he had gone to heaven to be with God.

"Grandpa was really looking forward to going to heaven. He had been praying and speaking to Jesus a lot, he just really wanted to be with Him forever."

"Did God know that you were sad about Grandpa?"

"Yes, he did. He knows everything. I spoke to God a lot and told Him how sad I was feeling. God always listens."

"Why did God let Grandpa die then if he knew you were so sad?"

"Well Jake, it's like I told you. Everyone and everything has to die. Because human beings sinned, did wrong things and kept disobeying God, everything has to die. Grandpa had to die someday and God knew the best time for it to happen. We all felt really sad, but it was good to know that God understood and that he still cared for all of us."

"How does God understand?" Jake was full of questions.

"God knows what it is like to be sad. He knows what it is like to have someone you love die. Jesus was God's only son and he died so that when we die we can go to live with him, for ever, in heaven.

But when Jesus was living on earth he also had a special friend who died. It made Jesus very sad."

Mum sat down on a bench and Jake and Tammy sat down beside her.

"It happened like this. Jesus was on a journey and a messenger came from his friends, Mary and Martha. They lived in a town called Bethany. Well the message was that Lazarus their brother was very sick and about to die.

"Mary and Martha were really worried and they asked Jesus to come to Bethany to make Lazarus better. Jesus had power over death and illness because he was the Son of God.

Well, when Jesus arrived in Bethany Lazarus was already dead. Everyone was really upset.

"Mary and Martha went to the grave with Jesus and when Jesus saw Lazarus' grave he cried.

"Everybody knew how much he loved Lazarus.

"Then Jesus did an amazing thing. He told some people to move away the stone and then he prayed. After he had prayed to God, his Father, Jesus shouted out in a loud voice, 'Lazarus come out!' What do you think happened? Lazarus came out of the grave. Jesus had made him live again. It was a miracle.

"Mary and Martha must have been so happy to have their brother alive again. How thankful they must have been to Jesus for helping them."

Tammy wanted to know why Jesus didn't stop everyone from dying.

"Why doesn't he get everyone to come out of their graves like he did for Lazarus?"

"Well, Lazarus had to die one day. Jesus took him back to life that day but one day, later on, Lazarus died and went to heaven. Everyone has to die. Jesus took Lazarus back to life to show us how powerful God is.

"It was a special miracle. Jesus did it for special reasons. He doesn't do it all the time because if he did then nobody would die. Death is something that happens to everyone. If the people that love God didn't die then they wouldn't get to heaven to be with him. God wants his friends to come to heaven to be with him and his son Jesus Christ. He knows that that is the best place for his friends.

"And one day, at the end of time, Jesus will make all our bodies alive again. That day has a special name. It is called the Judgement Day."

"Why is it called that Mum?" asked Jake.

"It's called the Judgement Day because that is the day when all the people who ever lived will come face to face with God and be judged by him. He will take the bodies of the people who love and trust in him into heaven and those who don't love and trust him will not be allowed in."

Jake looked at all the graves. There were lots of them. "Will all these bodies come back to life then too?"

"Yes, and they will be different, special bodies. These bodies will be bodies that last forever and that will never die again. Grandpa will come out of his grave and he won't have his sore hip anymore. He will be able to see perfectly. All the tired and broken bits will be mended... and his body will be reunited with the soul or spirit part of him in heaven. All of him, body and soul will be in heaven with Jesus for ever. That will be a joyful day for those who love God and a terrible day for those who don't love God."

As Jake looked again at all the graves, laid out in neat rows, he wondered about the people who had been buried here. How many of them had loved God and how many hadn't? It was too late now for those people who hadn't loved God. It was a sad thought.

"Does everybody get buried here, Mum?" Tammy asked.

"No, not everyone. There are other cemeteries. Some people don't get buried at all. They get cremated. Their bodies are burnt up instead of buried.

"Sometimes people's bodies can't be found - for example if they die in an accident at sea. But it doesn't matter how or when someone dies. God always knows what has happened. He never loses anybody who trusts in him.

"So, whatever happens, if you die loving and trusting in Jesus you will always be safe. It's important to trust in Jesus as he is the only way to heaven. If you don't love him then you don't get in."

"Sometimes children die Mum," whispered Jake.

"Yes, it is very sad when that happens.

But God loves to save children too. Jesus says that heaven is full of children."

"So Jesus is in heaven with lots of people and lots of children?"

"Yes, that's right."

"What do they do all day?"

"Well, I don't know exactly. They are very happy. They love God so much that they do a lot of singing and praising to God. It's a very wonderful place to be. We will just have to wait to get there before we know for sure what it is like.

"But because Jesus is there we know it is the best place to be. There's no pain there, no wickedness, no anger. "

"Wow!" said Tammy. "That's great."

When they got back to the big iron gates, Jake turned to take another look at his Grandpa's stone. He could still see it in the distance, tucked in beside a holly bush.

A bird was singing in the green holly bush. Jake thought this place was a very quiet place. It was very peaceful.

"I should write Grandma a letter to tell her I've seen Grandpa's grave. Do you think she'll like that Mum?"

"I think that would make her very happy. We'll buy a card at the shops," Mum said. "Oh and look Tammy, Jake - here's another bus we can catch."

Jake dashed out the iron gates and waved at the driver who stopped the bus and let them on.

Jacob Frances
Taylor
born 1930 died 1991
A loving husband
to
Martha and father
to
Jane and Matthew

Getting the Groceries

When they arrived at the supermarket Mum asked Jake, "Can you find a trolley Jake, while I help Tammy tie her shoelace?"

Jake dashed off to find one that didn't have a broken wheel. If the trolley had a broken wheel it made shopping very difficult and slow.

Trolleys with broken wheels would go all over the place and keep bumping into people.

Jake tried one trolley and put it back - it's back wheel was going all over the place. Then he pulled out another trolley and tried it out. It was just right.

Jake pushed it over to his mum.

"This one's fine Mum. It doesn't wobble at all."

Mum took hold of the trolley and they soon started to fling in the groceries as Mum began to charge round the supermarket.

Jake thought Mum was like a racing driver when she got going with her trolley.

He ran around after her while Tammy ran on in front. Tammy and Jake liked to pretend they were in a motor car race. Tammy made some good screeching and braking sounds as they ran past the pile of baked bean tins.

Tammy shouted, "Watch out for the lemonade bottles," as all three of them drove round a corner really fast. "Phew we just missed them," laughed Mum. Jake screeched to a stop. He was pretending

that his engines were making very loud noises. Tammy burst out giggling again. Her golden hair was all over the place and her cheeks were pink and flushed.

"Come on Mum you're not going fast enough!" Tammy pleaded.

But Mum was feeling a bit tired with all the running about and wanted to go a bit slower now. "Tammy, what about my eggs? They'll be all smashed."

But Mum still had lots of things to organise. She had a huge list of shopping to get and she needed to do some baking tonight. Jake wasn't sure why. Perhaps there was something special happening?

"Oh! Run back to that pile of baked beans and grab a tin for me Tammy dear," Mum said and Tammy dashed back to get one. Catching up with them a minute later, Tammy leaned over the trolley and dropped the tin of beans inside.

Mum was careful that Tammy didn't drop the tin of beans on top her eggs because that would make a very big mess.

"Get some apples for me Jake and Tammy reach up and get some of those carrots. I'll get some runner beans."

Jake grimaced, he hated runner beans. Mum saw his face and said, "Runner beans are good for you!"

Jake didn't bother to argue. Mum looked down her list of shopping and ticked off everything that they had put in the trolley.

"We've got flour and eggs and milk and apples. Did we get runner beans?"

"Yes!" said Jake, annoyed. "We got plenty of runner beans."

"Right then, we've got everything as far as I can see. I think we're ready to go

to the check out. Oh... before we forget...
Jake, you were going to get a card for
Grandma. Go and choose one while
Tammy helps me with the groceries."

Tammy and Mum picked up all the
groceries one by one and placed them on
the counter. Jake chose his card - one
with flowers on it - Grandma would like
that and then he placed it on the counter
too. The cashier pressed a button and
the groceries moved up the conveyer belt.
Each item was placed under a scanner
and a price appeared on the computer
screen above their heads.

Jake looked at all the different numbers
as they appeared on the screen. Because

it was a big shop there were lots of numbers for the machine to count. The numbers were coming so fast Jake couldn't count them for himself.

The cashier smiled at Jake as she kept scanning all the groceries. After she scanned one item she would place it down on the other side of the counter. Mum would then pick it up and put it in the shopping bag.

The cashier took a packet of beans and the machine went "beep", she took the apples, weighed them and then the machine went "beep" again.

Jake looked at the computer screen. Every time a grocery item went through the machine the big total at the bottom of the screen got bigger and bigger.

The runner beans went through the till and the machine went beep. Jake turned up his nose at the runner beans but he noticed that the total had increased again, and then when the crisps went through the total increased some more.

Jake was good at numbers and sums and he was sure Mum was spending more money than she normally did.

He looked at the pile of groceries still to go through the machine.

"Mum's spending a lot of money today," thought Jake.

Once the groceries were packed away Mum checked the total and sighed. "Oh well, we do have guests coming at the weekend. That's why it's so expensive."

Jake then remembered. Uncle Matthew and Auntie Clare were coming up for the weekend.

It was Uncle Matthew's birthday and Mum had asked him and Auntie Clare to come for a birthday tea. Mum was going to make a special meal. That was why

Mum had bought some nice ice-cream and some chocolate mint sweets.

Jake then remembered the runner beans and hoped they wouldn't have to eat them, but then he remembered that Mum would also bake a cake. She had bought some more flour and eggs and all sorts of other ingredients to bake the birthday cake with. That was definitely something to look forward to.

Jake looked again at the receipt and saw the number at the bottom.

"That's a lot of money Mum," he said.

"Yes, you're right Jake, but we don't always spend that much. It's a special occasion."

"Did that money come out of your bank then Mum?"

"Yes, Jake, somebody has to pay it. We've taken all these groceries from the shop. They wouldn't be pleased if we took all these things and didn't pay for them."

Mum thought a little and then remembered something. "I told you about Jesus Christ taking the punishment for our sin didn't I Jake?"

"Yes," Jake said, puzzled again. What more was Mum going to say?

"I just thought that when Jesus died, it was like he was paying a very big price. What if I had gone into the shop today and put all that food in my trolley but when I got to the check out I didn't have any money in the bank to pay for it all? What would I have done then?"

Jake shrugged his shoulders.

"I think you'd have been in trouble, Mum," said Tammy.

"Yes, that's right. You see we're in trouble because we've disobeyed God. When we sin it's like we have a big amount of money to pay but we don't have any money in our purse. We're in a lot of trouble. We've done all these bad things and have to be punished for them.

"Every time you sin, you disobey God. When Jesus asks you to trust in him it's just as though he is saying, 'Let me pay the price. Let me take your punishment instead and you can start again.' When you trust Jesus you are forgiven."

"Does that mean forgiven forever Mum?" asked Jake.

"Yes it does."

"What if I'm forgiven and then the next day I do something wrong. Does God get angry with me again?"

"If you trust in Jesus you are forgiven forever, but something else happens. When you trust in Jesus you change. The bit inside that always wanted to do bad things starts to become better. Jesus helps you to be a better person. You start to want to please God more and when you sin, you are sorry for it.

"You will never be perfect as long as you live on earth. The only time you stop doing bad things is when you go to heaven. And the only way to get to heaven is...?"

"By trusting in Jesus Christ," Tammy and Jake said together.

"Correct! Now, thankfully Dad is coming to pick us up in his car so we don't have to go back on the bus. He won't be long but lets have a milkshake while we wait."

Jake chose a strawberry milkshake. Tammy chose a banana one. Mum was going to take a cup of tea but then she chose a chocolate milkshake instead.

Everyone really enjoyed drinking their shakes through their straws. When Jake finished his he made a loud sucking noise and then smacked his lips.

"Yum, yum! Strawberry milkshake is the best!"

As Tammy slowly finished her Banana milkshake she asked Mum a question.

"What happens to people if they don't listen to what God says?"

"Well Tammy. People who don't love God don't go to heaven when they die."

"That's a disaster isn't it?" said Jake.

"Yes, a very big disaster... and that reminds me of another story. It's a quick one so I'll be able to tell it to you before Dad arrives.

"Jesus was a very good story teller and one day he told the disciples a story about two builders.

"These two builders were planning to build new houses. One builder had all his material, the bricks and stones and everything and he chose to build his house on a good strong rock.

"However, it was a difficult job and he had to work very hard.

"Another builder had purchased stones

and rocks to build his house with but instead of building it on good, strong rock he built his house on sand. Perhaps he thought it would be easier and not such hard work to build his house on the sand.

"Anyway, one day both the houses were finished. That night a big storm blew up and the floods came and hit the houses. The house that stood on the rock was strong and firm because it was standing on good, strong, rock but the house on the sand had no strong foundations and it fell down flat.

"Jesus said that the builder who built his house on the rock is like the person who listens to what God says and obeys him. But the builder who built his house on the soft sand is like the person who doesn't do what God says. That person is very foolish and one day he will have a disaster, just like the builder who foolishly built his house on the sand."

Jake enjoyed that story. Just when it had finished Tammy spotted Dad's blue Fiesta car. "Dad's here. Dad's here," she shouted.

Quickly Mum gathered up the shopping.

Jake was glad it was time to go home. It had been a very busy day.

"We've had a bus ride, we visited Grandpa's grave, we've done shopping, had a milkshake and lots of stories. Phew, I'll be glad when it's time for tea. I wonder what's on the television tonight?"

Watching the Television

Jake and Tammy settled down that night to eat some pizza and salad by the television. They watched some cartoons and then they watched a story about a dog who rescued some children from a burning house.

"It was amazing about that dog, Mum wasn't it?" Jake exclaimed. Jake wondered if Dogger would ever do something as brave as that dog did.

"Yes, it was very clever of that dog to wake up the owners. He didn't stop barking until he knew they were awake."

Tammy had enjoyed the story too, especially as it had had a happy ending.

"The dog didn't get hurt did he Mum?" she asked, just to be sure.

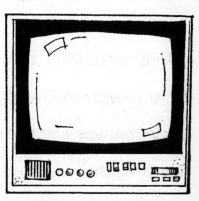

"No I don't think he got hurt because his owner managed to lift him out the window when the firemen came. But I remember a story that my dad once told me about a fire. Do you want to hear it?"

Jake switched the television off and Tammy and he settled down to hear Mum's story.

"Well one day Grandpa was in a hotel. He was on a business trip and had some belongings in a suitcase. As well as his clothes and other things he had some photographs of Grandma and me and Uncle Matthew which he liked to take with him when he went away. It meant that he didn't feel so homesick.

"He also had some important papers for his meetings the next day and they were in his briefcase.

"When it was time to go to bed that night he placed his wallet beside the brief case and his watch. He really liked his watch as it was one that he had got as a birthday present many years before from his own daddy. It was a special watch.

"Anyway, once Grandpa was asleep in bed, a fire started in the hotel kitchen. The cooks and the waiters tried to put it out, but it soon got too hot and they had to call the fire brigade. The smoke was so thick they could hardly breathe.

"There wasn't a fire alarm in the hotel, which was dangerous. The hotel staff had to run round all the guests rooms, knocking on the doors and warning them to get out of their beds.

'Wake up. Wake up,' they shouted through the key holes. 'There's a fire. You have to get out, or you will die.'

"The fire was getting very dangerous. Grandpa woke up with a start. He thought he had been dreaming. He waited for a minute and then he turned to go back to sleep. But just then he heard a knock on the bedroom door next to his and someone shouting, 'Get up! Get up! There's a fire!'

"Quickly Grandpa jumped out of his bed. 'What will I do? What will I do?' he thought. For a minute, Grandpa thought he would get into his clothes. He started to look for his shirt and trousers. But then he heard, the anxious voices of the hotel staff shouting, 'Everybody get out of the hotel. There's a fire. Get out now. It's very dangerous. Everybody out now.'

"Their voices were getting louder and louder. Grandpa realised that it must be very serious.

'I'd better go outside in my pyjamas,' he thought. 'But I'll take my wallet just in case and I don't want to leave my special watch.'

Tammy looked shocked, "Silly Grandpa, he should get out. Get out Grandpa now!"

Mum laughed, "Well when he started to look for his wallet and his watch he heard something else. It was one of the other hotel guests knocking on the door of his bedroom. The guest shouted out, 'Leave everything and get out now. The fire is really dangerous. Get out NOW!'

"Grandpa then felt really scared and he left everything in his room and ran out into the corridor. There was a smell of smoke. Lots of people were running down the corridor. Quickly he followed them. Some were trying to open the lift doors. Then someone shouted, 'Don't go down that way. It's too dangerous. The fire will trap you. Get out of the building by using the stairs.'

Grandpa moved to the stairs and quickly made his way down to the ground floor and out into the open air.

Lots of people were outside on the grass. Everybody was in their pyjamas. They had all left their possessions in their rooms.

"They realised that it would have been too dangerous to stay behind to get dressed or to find their wallets. If they had they might have died. Grandpa was relieved that he hadn't stayed behind to find his watch. Even though he lost his watch, his wallet, his papers, the photographs and his clothes, he was glad that he escaped with his life."

Jake's eyes were like saucers. "What an amazing story Mum. Did that really happen to Grandpa?"

"Yes, Jake it did. I was only a little girl when it happened. When Grandpa came home and told us about what had happened, I was so glad that he was home safe. Grandpa was too and he thanked God for looking after him and for saving his life.

Life is a precious gift and Grandpa realised this. He was glad to get home and to see his family again. It didn't matter that he had lost the photographs, he would get other ones taken. It didn't matter that he had lost his watch. We got him another one for his birthday. Grandpa was alive and that was what mattered.

Our possessions and clothes and things are not that important. Our lives are more important and so are our souls. Our hands and faces and legs and things are amazing. We should thank God for giving them to us. But the special bit of us, our soul, is even more precious. We should look after it by trusting and obeying God."

Grandpa's Story

Later on while Dad was out mowing the lawn, Tammy and Jake started to get ready for bed. After they had got into their pyjamas Mum allowed them to come downstairs for a cup of cocoa. Tammy wanted a goodnight kiss from Dad, who was just cleaning up the lawn mower.

"He won't be long now Tammy. Just be

patient. While we're waiting I'll tell you another story. When Grandpa came home after the fire he read this story to me from the Bible."

"What story was that Mum?"

"Well when Grandpa was sitting out in the cold on the grass he was watching the firemen pour water onto the fire. He was looking at all the people shivering and then he realised that all the people on the grass had been very wise to leave their clothes and things behind. If they hadn't the fire might have trapped them and they would have been very foolish.

"However, Grandpa thought that everybody looked rather funny standing around in their night clothes. They were all out in the cold with nowhere else to go. It reminded him a little bit about the story of the ten bridesmaids. Jesus told a story once about ten bridesmaids who were getting ready for a wedding."

Mum picked up her Bible and flicked through the pages until she found the story that she was looking for.

"In Jesus' country bridesmaids were given the job of walking with the bridegroom to the wedding feast.

"The ten bridesmaids had to wait for the bridegroom to get ready and when he was ready they would then go with him. It didn't matter what time of the day or night the bridegroom came the bridesmaids would have to be ready for him.

"However, not all of the ten bridesmaids were ready. Five of the bridesmaids were. They were wise. Five of the bridesmaids weren't ready. They were foolish.

"The five wise bridesmaids had made sure that their lamps had plenty of oil in them, just in case the bridegroom came at night. If he did come at night the wise bridesmaids had realised that they would have to have lamps to light their way along the dark streets. But the five foolish bridesmaids hadn't thought of this and had forgotten to make sure that their lamps had plenty of oil.

"Later that night the bridesmaids were woken up with a shout. 'The bridegroom is here. Go out to meet him.'

"The five wise bridesmaids got out their lamps and lit them but the five foolish bridesmaids didn't have enough oil. They couldn't light their lamps.

'Oh, bother. Give us some of your oil,' they asked their friends.

'No, we can't,' their friends said, 'or we won't have enough oil for ourselves. Go to the market and buy some more.' The five foolish bridesmaids ran off to get some more oil and the five wise bridesmaids walked with the bridegroom to the wedding feast.

"By the time the five foolish bridesmaids had returned from the market, they were too late. The bridegroom had gone into the wedding feast with his bride and the five wise bridesmaids. The doors were locked and nobody else was going to be allowed in. The foolish bridesmaids pleaded to be let in but the bridegroom didn't know who they were and so they missed out on the party."

"That's a shame," said Tammy sadly.

"Yes, it is, Tammy," agreed Mum, "But the five foolish bridesmaids only had themselves to blame. They should have been ready. Then they would have got into the wedding feast. But missing out on heaven is far worse than missing out on a wedding. The foolish bridesmaids got locked out of the wedding because they weren't ready. If you don't trust Jesus and aren't ready to die, then you risk being locked out of heaven. If you die without loving Jesus, then you cannot go to heaven to be with him."

Mum put down the Bible

"Remember how I told you that everyone dies one day?"

Tammy nodded.

"Can you remember what happens to people who die not believing in Jesus?"

Jake nodded, "They don't go to heaven.

They go to hell instead and that's a horrible place because Jesus isn't there. There isn't any love there."

"That's right. Hell is a place we have to escape from. Hell is a place of punishment. But heaven is a place of joy and that is a place that we really, really want to go to.

"The five foolish bridesmaids wanted to go somewhere, didn't they? They wanted to go to the wedding feast. But they couldn't get in because they hadn't been ready.

"We want to go to heaven when we die but we have to be ready. We have to be friends with Jesus. We have to ask God to forgive us for all the sins and bad things we have done. If we do this we will be ready to go to heaven when we die. If we don't then we won't be ready and we will be locked out."

Just then Dad wandered in.

"Is it story time then?" he asked.

"Yes," said Tammy. "We had a story about five foolish bridesmaids."

"Oh, that one. I remember that story. But do you know what my favourite story is, said Dad.

"No. What is it?" Jake asked.

"It's the story about when 5,000 people weren't ready, but two people were."

"5,000 - that's a huge number," gasped

Jake. He had never done a sum with such a big number in it, ever.

"What did the 5,000 people forget to do?" asked Tammy.

"Well," smiled Dad, "they forgot to bring their lunches with them to a picnic."

"That was silly. They must have been very hungry," exclaimed Tammy.

"Extremely hungry," said Dad. "Only one little boy had a picnic with him. Do you want to know what was in it?"

Jake nodded. He licked his lips as he thought about his favourite picnic food - cheese and pickle sandwiches. Dad then told his story.

"The boy had five loaves of bread and

two fish. Quite a small picnic really, but I'm sure the boy was pleased. Nobody else had any food with them.

"When the disciples started speaking to Jesus about the problem of all these people and no food, the little boy started to think. He decided that he wanted to give his picnic to Jesus as he would know what to do with it.

"When Jesus asked his disciples if there was any food, one disciple, called Andrew told him that there was a boy who had a picnic - five loaves and two fish, 'But how will we feed 5,000 people with just five loaves and two fish, Jesus?'

"Jesus knew what he was doing. He

was ready too. He took the food and thanked God for it. Then he started to break it up. By the end of the day everybody had had more than enough to eat. Jesus fed the 5,000 people who had forgotten their lunches, all from five loaves and two fish.

"There was even a whole pile of leftovers to take home. What a miracle!"

"That's amazing," Jake gasped.

"Yes, it reminds me of how loving and caring Jesus is. Even if you know you aren't ready to go to heaven, all you have to do is ask Jesus to help you. Just as he helped the people who didn't have their lunches with them, Jesus will help you to get to heaven. He is the only one who can do it - he is the only one you should ask to help you get into heaven. Now who wants me to tuck them up into bed?"

Tammy yawned and then sleepily said, "Yes, and don't forget to give me my good night kiss!"

Mum smiled, "And don't you forget to brush your teeth!"

Uncle Matthew's Birthday Party

It wasn't long before the weekend and the day of Uncle Matthew's birthday party. Mum was really busy, cleaning and tidying. She started in the kitchen after breakfast and then she went into the living room with her duster. She polished the clock and dusted the bookshelves.

July

S	M	T	W	T	F	S
31					1	2
3	4	5	6	7	8	9
10	11	12	13	14	15	16
17	18	19	20	21	22	23
24	25	26	27	28	29	30

Even Dad had an apron on and was cleaning out the kitchen bin in the back garden. All sorts of mucky stuff was stuck to the bottom of it. Tammy took one sniff of the smelly old bin and ran upstairs to tidy out her shelves. "Pooh!" she said.

Jake couldn't believe that there were so many places that needed tidying. What a bore! The tops of the doors even got dusted. Mum told Jake to tidy his room. Sighing he went and looked at his toys and books all over the floor.

"Oh well," he said, "I'll shove the toys under the bed and put the books in this box."

Jake couldn't be bothered sorting his

books back onto the shelf. Putting the toys back into the toy box was too much like hard work. Jake did find some smelly socks and an old t-shirt under the bed but instead of putting them in the laundry basket Jake just left them under the bed and then went down stairs again.

"Finished Mum. Can I go out and play?"

"What?" exclaimed Mum. "Already? Are you sure? I'm coming up to check."

Jake looked a little uncomfortable. He had put all the things away. He thought the room looked tidy, but he wasn't sure if Mum would think the same way.

Mum came into the bedroom and looked around. There were no toys on the floor and no books to be seen. Mum looked at the bookshelf where the books were supposed to be, then she knew what Jake had done.

With one step she strode over to the bed and lifted up the bed spread. She nudged the pile underneath and a huge pile of toys and books and dirty laundry tumbled out onto the bedroom floor.

"Jake!" Mum gasped. "This room is NOT

tidy. You are not going out to play until it is finished, and I mean finished. Tidy the toys into the toy box, the books onto the shelf, the dirty laundry into the laundry basket and then I want you to take the duster, and polish all the surfaces. I told you to dust in here yesterday. You haven't done it."

Jake looked ashamed. Mum had told him to dust his shelves when they came back from their shopping trip. But his favourite television programme had been on and instead of polishing he had watched the television and forgotten all about the dusting. Mum had telescopic eyes when it came to dust. She never missed a speck.

Tammy peeked in the door as Jake started to sort the toys and books. Jake didn't speak to her as he was sulking.

He was still sulking when the door bell rang. He was still sulking when Uncle Matthew and Auntie Clare came up to say hello. He was still sulking when Mum served tea in the kitchen.

She had her best plates out and there was cake for afters but Jake still sulked. He was really angry when Mum told him to stop being silly and eat his runner beans. He got so angry that he stamped his foot and shouted "It's not fair."

Dad told him to go to his room immediately and Jake ran upstairs crying. What a horrible day. Everything had gone wrong.

Jake sulked and sulked. He lay on his bed and kicked off the bedspread. His eyes were dark and gloomy and his mouth was turned down at the corners. He looked out the window and saw the big tree standing in the garden still and quiet. He watched the hundreds of little green leaves, shimmering and dancing in the breeze and he remembered the questions about death.

He remembered how death had all started long long ago and how everything had gone wrong and horrible, just like his day.

He remembered that Adam and Eve had disobeyed God and then it had all gone wrong.

Jake remembered how he had disobeyed his mum by not tidying his room. That was when today had all gone wrong.

Then Jake thought, "I wasn't disobeying Mum, I was disobeying God." Jake felt awful. That was so wrong. He knew that because of that wrong thing and all the other wrong things he had done, like hitting Tammy and breaking the vase and lying about it - he wouldn't go to heaven when he died. He wanted to go to heaven. This whole thing made him feel really sad and really horrible.

But just then Mum and Tammy came in the door. Tammy was holding a plate with a slice of cake on it. When Jake saw Mum he jumped out of bed and said, "I'm sorry

Mum. I'm really sorry. I don't want to be bad anymore I want to be good. I've been really horrible and I broke your vase it wasn't Dogger, it was me." Jake burst into tears. Tammy looked as if she might cry too and her nose even started to dribble. Mum quickly found a piece of tissue to wipe Tammy's nose and then she settled Jake and Tammy down on the bed. Jake shoved his big brown bear out of the way to make room for everybody.

"Do you remember what I said about being good Jake?" Mum looked into Jake's eyes. Jake could see that she wasn't angry with him, just concerned. Jake was relieved to know that his mum still loved him. Mum asked the question again. "Do you remember what I said about being good? You can't do it on your own. You have to have Jesus to help you.

"You see, once when Jesus was alive there was a very nasty man called Zaccheus. He was really horrible. Zaccheus was a rotten cheat. He stole money from people and nobody could do anything about it.

"There was one other thing about Zaccheus, as well as being very nasty, he was very small. So small infact, that if he was behind you in a crowd, he couldn't see over your head. And one day Zaccheus really wanted to see someone who was going to come to his town that day. It was Jesus. But Zaccheus couldn't get to the front of the crowd and he was too small to see over everybody.

"Zaccheus the nasty cheat was in a spot of bother until he spotted a big tree."

"Was it as big as our tree Mum?" Tammy asked.

"I don't know Tammy, but it was pretty big. Big enough to be able to see the whole street from, if you climbed up into its branches. Quickly Zaccheus climbed up it and was really pleased that he was now taller than everyone else and could see Jesus walking along the road.

"To his surprise, Jesus stopped right

below his tree and looked up at him. Jesus then asked Zaccheus if he could come to his house. Zaccheus was overjoyed. Everyone else was annoyed. They didn't like to see Jesus going to visit the house of that nasty old cheat.

"But when Jesus came to Zaccheus' house Jesus changed Zaccheus. Zaccheus believed and trusted in Jesus and told Jesus that he would stop cheating and would pay back the money to all the people he had stolen from. It wasn't because Zaccheus was a good man that he did this, it was because Jesus Christ changed Zaccheus' heart. When you trust in Jesus Christ he changes you on the inside. Just like Zaccheus you won't want to sin anymore and Jesus Christ will help you. Do you want to do that Jake? Do you?"

Jake sighed quietly. He snuggled up to his mum and she gave him a quick hug.

Jake looked out the window once again. A bird was singing on one of the branches of the big green tree. Jake then knew that he had to. Jake knew that Jesus was the only person who could take him to heaven. If he trusted in him he needn't be afraid of death anymore.

What do you think?

Jake

What do you think Jake will do? He wants to be good. He knows that the only way to be good is to trust in Jesus. When he trusts in Jesus Christ Jake knows that Jesus will change him. He will make Jake a friend of God and also help him to start obeying God. Jake also knows that the only way to get to heaven and to be with God forever is to trust in Jesus.

What would you do?

Tammy

Tammy has learnt a lot about life and death - have you? Tammy was worried about the little bird at the beginning of this story. What things worry you about life? Do you worry about school or about falling out with your friends? Tammy didn't like to think about death. But Mum told her and Jake about how trusting in Jesus Christ means we can have everlasting life. Jesus wants to save you.

Have you asked him to do this?

Life and Death

It's important to remember that everything is under God's control. Even when things don't happen the way we want them to. Even when sad and bad times come Jesus Christ is always there for us. Nothing happens in life or in death that he can't handle. He is our best and most loving friend. We can talk to him at any time and he will always listen. He longs to comfort people with sad hearts. Jesus knows what it is like to cry. He knows how horrible death is. But if you

trust in him and love him with all your heart you will find out how wonderful life can be. He will give you everlasting life in heaven with him when you die.

"Believe in the Lord Jesus Christ and you will be saved." Acts 16:31

Look out for other titles in this series:

The Dark Blue Bike at Number Seventeen
Tammy and Jake learn about
Friendship and Bullying

Jake's best friend has left the area and Jake
is feeling down in the dumps about the
whole thing. On the first day back at School
Jake decides to play truant with disasterous
results. Find out about Daniel the school bully,
his fantastic new bike and his mysterious trips
into London with his father.
The children of Canterbury Place have a lot
to learn about bullies and what to do about
them as well as what a real friend Jesus is.

The Deep Black Pond at Number Twelve
Tammy and Jake learn about
Health and Sickness

Tammy and Jake are helping out Joyce in
her garden... and it needs a lot of help. The
weeds are everywhere and the soil is really
rocky. It is in great need of some tender
loving care. Daniel's mum is also in need of
care as her illness continues to worry Daniel
and his friends.
The children of Canterbury place have a lot
to learn about health and what a gift it is
from God.

Ten Boys who changed the World

Would you like to change your world? These ten boys grew up to do just that:

Billy Graham, Brother Andrew, John Newton, George Muller, Nicky Cruz, William Carey, David Livingstone, Adoniram Judson, Eric Liddell, Luis Palau.

Find out how Eric won the race and honoured God; David became an explorer and explained the Bible; Nicky joined the gangs and then the church; Andrew smuggled Bibles into Russia and brought hope to thousands and John captured slaves but God used him to set them free.

Find out what God wants you to do!

ISBN: 1-85792-579-3

LIGHT
KEEPERS

Ten Girls who changed the World

Would you like to change your world? These ten girls grew up to do just that:

Isobel Kuhn, Elizabeth Fry, Amy Carmichael, Gladys Aylward, Mary Slessor, Catherine Booth, Jackie Pullinger, Evelyn Brand, Joni Eareckson Tada, Corrie Ten Boom.

Find out how Corrie saved lives and loved Jesus in World War II; Mary saved babies in Africa and fought sin; Gladys rescued 100 children and trusted God; Joni survived a crippling accident and thanked Jesus; Amy rescued orphans and never gave up; Isobel taught the Lisu about Christ; Evelyn obeyed God in India; Jackie showed love in awful conditions in Hong Kong; Elizabeth helped prisoners; and Catherine rolled up her sleeves and helped the homeless!

Find out what God wants you to do!

ISBN: 1-85792-649-8

Rainforest Adventures
Amazon Adventures

The Amazon Rainforest is the oldest and largest rain forest in the world. Covering a huge area of South America it has the most varied plant and animal habitat on the planet. Read this book and you will join an expedition into the heart of the rain forest.

Discover the tree frog's nest, the chameleon who can change it's colour and the very hungry piranha fish. Even the possum can teach a lesson about speaking out for Jesus Christ and the parasol ant can show us how to keep going and not give up. Then there's the brightly coloured toucan whose call reminds us that with God we can do anything. Discover what its like to actually live in the Rain forest. Join in the adventures and experience the exciting and dangerous life of a pioneer missionary in South America.

ISBN: 1-85792-627-7
ISBN: 1-85792-440-1

Sarah & Paul

Written by Derek Prime

Find out about the Christian Faith with these stories of the Sarah and Paul and their friends.

Sarah & Paul
go back to *School*
Discover about God and the Bible
ISBN 1 87167 6185

Sarah & Paul
have a *Visitor*
Discover the Lord Jesus
ISBN 1 87167 6193

Sarah & Paul
go to the *Seaside*
Discover the Holy Spirit and the Church
ISBN 1 87167 6347

Sarah & Paul
make a *Scrapbook*
Discover the Lord's Prayer
ISBN 1 87167 6355

Sarah & Paul
go to the *Museum*
Discover the ten Commandments
ISBN 1 87167 6363

Sarah & Paul
on *Holiday Again*
Discover about becoming a Christian
ISBN 1 87167 6371

How to handle your life and other helpful hints from God

by Carine Mackenzie

Are you the kind of person that likes to have answers, solutions or at least clues to what is going on in your life? Is your brain in knots wondering about why things always happen to you? Why is it that things never seem to go the way you plan?

Well sit back, unwind your mind and get into the daily habit of talking to someone about all these knotty problems and difficulties you have. God is ready to listen and has ready-made advice - just for you!

Throughout this book you will find short snappy stories and mind bending puzzles to get you thinking - but as well as that you will find out loads of things about God.

What does God think about fashion? Family? Friends? What about all my plans that keep going wrong? What does God want me to do? What does the Bible say... and that's another important thing... Look out for the Bible reading pages and prayer points. Use them well and you will find that you have started something excellent!

ISBN 1-85792-520-3

CHRISTIAN FOCUS

Good books with the real message of hope!

Christian Focus Publications publishes biblically-accurate books for adults and children.

If you are looking for quality Bible teaching for children then we have a wide and excellent range of Bible story books - from board books to teenage fiction, we have it covered.

You can also try our new Bible teaching Syllabus for 3-9 year olds and teaching materials for pre-school children.

These children's books are bright, fun and full of biblical truth, an ideal way to help children discover Jesus Christ for themselves. Our aim is to help children find out about God and get them enthusiastic about reading the Bible, now and later in their lives.

Find us at our web page:
www.christianfocus.com